The Tale
of Shu the Cat

GEORGE T. SPENCE

CONTENTS

Chapter 1   Pg 1

Chapter 2   Pg 3

Chapter 3   Pg 7

Chapter 4   Pg 9

Chapter 5   Pg 12

Chapter 6   Pg 15

Chapter 7   Pg 17

Chapter 8   Pg 19

Chapter 9   Pg 21

Chapter 10   Pg 23

Chapter 11   Pg 24

Chapter 12   Pg 27

Chapter 13   Pg 30

Chapter 14   Pg 31

Chapter 15   Pg 32

Chapter 16   Pg 34

ACKNOWLEDGMENTS

This story was born in Singapore in 1990 and is set
around a real home and real friends.

CHAPTER 1

Monna the cat was cold, hungry and very wet. She was one of the many wild cats roaming Singapore - wild in the sense that they were all descendants from domestic parents, but had never had a home to live in. They lived on scraps of food they found from people who left things out for them or from the refuge chutes that abound in Singapore. Of course they also had to hunt for food in the shape of small lizards, called geckos or chee chas or chit chats. They also hunted birds, insects or anything else they could find to fill their empty tummies.

Monna was dark brown in colour with black stripes and one small patch of white above her right eye. Nobody could say she was a pretty cat as her fur was lacking lustre and she was, or would have been, very thin except for the fact that she was due to give birth to kittens. Her stomach was heavily distended with the kittens she carried and she knew she was very near her time to bring her offspring into the world.

Monna was creeping, watchfully, through the jungle like growth that was in the tree area that surrounded a place called Goodwood Hill in downtown Singapore, near the busy main shopping area of the city. These jungle-like areas were numerous in Singapore as it is a tropical island and the areas were allowed to develop as naturally as a jungle forest would do, if left on its own. There were two roads passing through Goodwood Hill, just like English country lanes and from both these roads there were small lanes leading to houses, which were snuggled right up to the edges of the jungle areas. The houses, backyards and car parking clearances had been hacked out of the jungle growth and only the constant work of the occupants kept the growth at bay otherwise the jungle would, very quickly have resumed its rightful place and absorbed the cleared areas, houses and all. There was also all manner of tropical birds, lizards, insects and snakes in these jungle wooded areas but the snakes were not often seen by the occupants as the

1

government of Singapore made a great effort to make sure they were kept away from the rural districts of the city.

Monna knew all about these dangerous reptiles – dangerous to cats, dogs, birds and any other type of animal or fowl that lived in Singapore – but not dangerous to the people that lived in Singapore. Monna had watched her own mother being caught and eaten by a python when she was little older than a kitten herself and could still remember the terror that she had felt as her mother disappeared down the pythons throat. Yes! Monna knew how to be very careful and watchful wherever she was but especially when she was in an overgrown or wooded area.

As she crawled on through the heavy undergrowth, miserable and feeling so sorry for herself, she watched and listened very carefully. She knew she would have to find a warm, dry, safe place soon as she could feel her babies moving in her tummy. She stopped suddenly as she neared the end of the undergrowth because she could smell the humans and see the brightly light interior of the house where they stayed. She also caught the smell of cat but no scent of dogs. Monna thought about this, as she stood silently, with one paw raised, in the process of taking another step before she had frozen. If the humans have a cat they must like our kind she reasoned and if they do there might be some food around which the other cat didn't want. She stood very still, thinking about this, even though the rain water was still dripping from the trees and undergrowth into her already saturated fur. Miserable and hungry, she still wasn't taking any chances. A small "meeow" escaped through her lips as she felt the first birth pains hit her tummy. She knew then she had to find a warm, dry place to have her kittens quite quickly.

CHAPTER 2

Smudge cocked his ears up, sharply, as he thought he heard the sound of a "meeow" coming from another cat quite close to his home. He leapt down from his place on Tony's lap and strolled towards the front door of the house, looking back at Tony as if to say "Let me out please". "No you don't!" said Margot, Tony's wife, "You're not going out there tonight and then coming in here with yourself all muddy and wet. Don't you have the sense that GOD gave you to know it's still raining out there?" Tony laughed as he watched the comical expression on Smudge's face, which seemed to him to say "Ah women! Always making a fuss". Margot of course didn't expect an answer from Smudge but had asked the question anyway as if Smudge was more than just a cat. Smudge thought he would try a small "meeow" to see if that would help convince Tony or Margot to let him out – not that he really wanted to go out on a night like it was outside. "Get on your bike" said Margot laughingly, "you're not on!" Both Tony and Margot laughed even louder as Smudge looked at her, quite calmly, then stretched out his, well-rounded overweight body, unsheathed his claws and started pulling at Margot's good scatter rug which was nearest to him, knowing of course that he wasn't allowed to do this. "Smudge!" shouted Margot "If I've to come to you, you'll be in deep, deep trouble." Smudge decided it wasn't worth all this trouble and bother as he had not heard another sound from outside, so, he stopped clawing, sheathed his claws and jumped onto the couch, turning his back on his owners just to show them he was in the huff at not being allowed out. Tony had another chuckle to himself, then turned back to telling Margot how his day at the office had been.

Monna by this time had edged her way right to the edge of the house garden but had remained in the undergrowth. She had heard the noise from the house and the shout from Margot at Smudge so she was just as wary as ever about sniffing around but she was still very hungry and this place still looked like the best place she had seen.

The house was built on a small area levelled out of the sloping ground from the side of the road with trees close up to two faces of the house at the back and forward gable end. The front of the car porch there was a small tree clump which cars had to drive around to get to the parking area under the porch. The back gable of the house had a sloping roof extending down from the house going toward the annexed buildings, which were sitting on another piece of level ground on the sloping house grounds. The extended roof of the main house had been made into a covered walkway which was used as protection for anyone leaving the main house, going to the annexed rooms, from the rain that fell during what would have been the country's winter season. The rain, from the buildings roofs and tarmacked area, ran into small open drains, which overlapped at each section, going down the slope, causing miniature waterfalls, till it reached the bottom of the garden, just in front of Monna, where it flowed into the main monsoon ditch.

Monna could see the annexed building roofs were quite high but due to the main building roof being extended to be used as a covered walkway, it brought it very near to the natural slope of the ground, which hadn't been touched when the house was constructed. The roof was so near that a small climb up one of the trees and a small leap would get her onto the main house roof and that, she reasoned, would be where she would find any geckos that would still be active on a rainy night like this. Monna cautiously edged her way, passed the main monsoon ditch, passed the annex buildings, and moved up the slope toward the tree she had decided would provide her a means of climbing, for her jump onto the main building roof.

As she moved along she sniffed at all the likely places she thought would hide a scrap of food or a hiding gecko or insect. When she eventually reached her chosen tree, she saw it was going to be easy for her to get onto the roof and search for anything hiding up there which she could eat. Quickly she scrambled up the tree of her choice and onto the branch that extended over the roof, about one foot above. She picked her way along the branch and dropped, lightly, onto the roof of the covered walkway. As she stepped away from where she had landed, her eyes caught the quick movement of a lizard diving under the roof tiles, at the junction of the main house roof and the covered walkway tiles. Monna scampered over toward the spot where she had seen the small lizard vanish.

Investigation of the area revealed a space between the two roofs which had not been covered properly when the house had been built. As she advanced, Monna discovered a space deep enough to hold two cats, quite dry, rain and wind proof. She cautiously continued to enter this haven, looking for her first meal in two days, but there was no sign of the lizard. She sniffed around to see if there was anything else that she might eat, but had no success. Her hunger drove her on, so back into the dark, dismal night she went.

After an hour on the roof she had only managed to catch a very small gecko which only made her feel hungrier. Monna decided to go back to the ground to see if she could find any scraps of food that the cat who lived here had left uneaten. She lightly leapt up onto the branch overhanging the roof, and easily made her way down the sloping trunk of the tree, down to the ground. As she reached the base of the tree there was a flash of lightning, illuminating the trees and area surrounding the house. A peal of thunder crashed and echoed in the dark night sky. Monna was used to this in Singapore but never felt happy about it as she knew that this, usually, meant heavier rain which would make her even more wet and cold than she was at this moment.

Nervously she went forward from the tree base, still looking for something to eat, toward the main entrance to the house. Another flash of lightning zig-zagged its way across the rain soaked night sky. She froze! Was that a bird she had seen in the grass next to the clump of trees in the front of the car porch, around which the household car had to drive? The thunder rumbled away into the background again. Monna waited very tensely for the next flash of lightning, which would reveal the area, preparing herself for the leap that could be the difference between having a meal and going hungry again. It had been two days since her last small meal and she knew that this might be her last chance tonight to fill her empty stomach.

With the flash of lightning she pounced, but the bird never moved. The bird was on its side with its head back over its wings at a funny angle, obviously dead with a broken neck. This had been one of Smudge's triumphs that afternoon but when Margo had caught him trying to sneak the bird into the house, she had scolded him while taking the bird away from him. When he wasn't looking she had thrown it into the grass, outside the front door, where he wasn't likely to look. The bird was a great find for Monna as it was a reasonably fresh kill. Monna looked around to see if there was a dry place where she could eat.

The rain started to get heavier as she was searching. The rain soaked night clouds unloaded their rain drops in a constant sheet on the already wet land of Singapore. Monna decided to head for the one dark, warm, dry spot she had found in her two day journey, looking for a safe place to have her kittens. Monna raced for the tree that led to the roof of Tony and Margo's house, with the bird firmly held in her mouth.

More lightning and thunder helped her move quickly up the tree and into the safety of the hole beneath the roof tiles. She made her way as far back as she could from the entrance, lay down and began feeding on Smudge's catch of the day. Well content with her meal and finding a new home for her kittens – which would be arriving very shortly – Monna licked herself as dry as possible, curled up, and went to sleep as the tropical storm crashed outside.

CHAPTER 3

Margot saw Tony off to the office the following morning, and the morning sunshine promised a dry, warm day. She went back into the kitchen and prepared Smudge's meal, placing it on the open porch at the back of the house under the covered walkway, before going into her bedroom to prepare herself for another busy day shopping and meeting her many friends.

Smudge, who had been crawling around Margot's feet while his meal had been prepared, had some of his cat food from his dish but, not being too hungry, left most of it. He knew there was a stranger in his domain as he could catch its scent on the morning air. Sniffing around he followed Monna's scent to the base of the tree she had used to get to the roof. He really should follow this up he knew, but being such a heavy, well-fed, lazy cat, he decided not to bother climbing the tree as he wasn't very happy at tree climbing anyway, having got stuck in one a long time ago, and having to be rescued before he could get back down to the ground. No! He wasn't going to chance that again, so he strolled off toward the trees where he had caught that bird yesterday. This time he might get playing with it as Margot was obviously going out, leaving him to fend for himself today.

Monna, meanwhile, was lying well content with her new home and her two fine kittens. They had arrived in the early hours of the morning and were now snuggled, sleeping close to their mummy's tummy, where they had just finished their first meal of warm, rich milk. Monna was licking their soft, hairless bodies clean with her tongue and wondering what she should name them. She was hungry again but really didn't want to leave her new-born son and daughter. She could smell the cat food that Smudge had left as the rich gravy scent drifted up on the increasingly hot morning air. She knew it was almost below her home as she had heard Margo place it down and then the sounds of Smudge having some of his meal. The smell of it was beginning to make her mouth water. She had to eat as only by eating

7

could she produce milk nourishing enough to feed the hungry kittens that at the moment were sleeping peacefully beside her.

Monna decided to see what she could do about that lovely smell of food that drifted into the hole under the roofs eaves. Slowly easing herself away from her new family, she silently moved to the edge of her sheltered home and peered out. It was a lovely, sunlight day, with jewels of brilliant light being reflected from the rain drops that still lay on leaves of the trees and grass, but that with the heat of day would soon vanish.

Monna spied the movement of a dark and white haired cat as he slowly strolled towards the trees that were further away from her safe shelter. He was paying no attention to anything that was going on around him. He was even ignoring the birds that were flitting in and out of the trees ahead of him. The birds of course were watching him very closely but this was an old game that he played as, once out of their sight, he would creep round to his favourite place for trying to catch any birds that landed on the ground.

Monna watched Smudge closely, for that was who the dark and white cat was, and when she decided his concentration was only on the brightly coloured birds, she slipped out and quickly made her way to the ground. Still keeping a wary eye in the direction that Smudge had taken, Monna moved quietly to the plate of food that had been placed out for Smudge's breakfast on the porch. She quickly ate her fill, all the time watching for any movement that might suggest that Smudge was returning.

Having satisfied her hunger, Monna's thoughts went towards her need to drink. This was going to be a long, hot day and if she didn't drink now, after having left her new-born kittens, she knew that she would have to leave them again before dark and she might be seen by the humans who lived here. Monna thought she had better take advantage of her of having left her kittens already to go to the monsoon drain that she had passed at the bottom of the garden last night.

She silently crept down to the bottom of the garden till she reached the ditch just at the place where it vanished underground to end up, eventually, going into the main catchment for rain water from all over Singapore, before going into the sea. The monsoon ditches which fed the main catchment ditch usually had some water flowing in them as they surfaced in each garden before going back underground on their way to the catchment. Monna eased herself down into the ditch, just at the place where it vanished underground before resurfacing further down the area in the neighbour's gardens. The water would be cool here and Monna cautiously lapped her fill from the water which was protected from the sun's rays, keeping an eye open for anything that might attack her. When she was finished she swiftly made her way back up the garden, up the tree, onto the roof and into her new home, to place herself round her two kittens protectively.

CHAPTER 4

Smudge, meanwhile, watched quietly from his hiding place in a clump of grass, which covered him from sight of the birds, hoping that one of them would come down from the trees, within leaping distance. No birds ventured down today as they had had a fright yesterday when they had watched Smudge catch one of their friends when he had sprung from an unknown place. No! Not one of them would leave their roosting tree for another two or three days until the memory of yesterday had faded like the mist at dawn with the rising of the sun.

Smudge began to feel hungry around midday and crept quietly away from his previous day's triumph's observation post, back towards his breakfast plate on the porch. The nearer he got to the porch and his meal the more he began to pick up the scent of the stranger. He could tell now that it was a female she-cat who had recently given birth to kittens and her scent was getting stronger and stronger the nearer he got to the house porch where his breakfast plate was. With a little run and a leap he was soon gazing down at his empty breakfast plate. His anger raised the hair, partially, on his back and a "meeow" of frustration came from deep inside his throat.

"How could she do this to me?" he raged. She was the intruder in his area and she had no right to leave him feeling hungry. Smudge quickly went to the tree that he knew the strange she-cat had used to climb up and down. He quickly scanned the tree and branches for a sign of her but found nothing. Again he wanted to scramble up that tree to find out where she had gone but again his old fear of trees kept his feet firmly planted on the ground.

A cricket was unlucky enough to pick that particular time to land at the bottom of the tree roots. Smudge lashed out, killing the cricket, with a "take that" swipe of his right paw. He felt better after he had eaten the cricket,

9

and wandered off to see if there were any more that he could catch and play with. It was good fun chasing them around as they tried to get away, he still felt angry but regained his peace of mind slowly.

At the 20ft wide, 10ft deep main catchment drain, the water was almost to the top as all the monsoon drains fed the water from rain-soaked Singapore into it. Numerous things had died in its troubled waters that night and earlier on in the morning but now a young python, about three feet in length, was struggling to get out of the clutches of the water flowing to the sea. He had been in one of the monsoon ditches, with others of his family, hiding and trying to find a dry place to rest when the torrent of rain water from the previous night's storm caught him and swept him from his precarious position within his drain, into the main catchment drain.

He was becoming exhausted with his struggles to keep his head above the water and get out of the current which held him in its grasp. He spied a tree branch racing down on him and as he got bumped, it pushed him from the fast moving water into the sluggish water near the side. A small, badly-built outcrop of cement on the side of the catchment, below one of the feeder monsoon drains, helped as well as it caused the slow-moving water to become calm in its move toward the sea.

The young python took advantage of this and slithered, thankfully, into the darkness of the drain, where only a little water now flowed, and moved confidently, happy but exhausted, further into the drain away from the dangerous, drowning, water forces that had pulled and tugged at him and almost succeeded in making him give up his fight to get back to dry land.

His body temperature was low, making him sluggish and slow in his movements but he knew that a few hours in the sunshine and heat would help him regain his speed. Continuing up the dark, dank, wet drain away from the catchment water, he sensed movement ahead of him, hurrying away from his slow approach. His senses told him that food was before him if he could just corner it.

The young rat ran frantically searching for a means of escape from the python it knew was coming towards him. He knew that if he didn't escape from this drain he might become a meal for the python just like the rest of his family had. He didn't know that this was another python and assumed it was the same one that had got his brothers and sisters in the drain where he had lived. Just like the young python he had been swept from his own home and had just arrived in his drain an hour before the python. Inexperience made him shoot into the first home he found between joints in the tunnel to the world above. As he scampered along the tunnel he could still hear the snake behind him and when he found the tunnel came to a dead end he knew his days were numbered. He desperately scratched the unfinished tunnel end as he heard the snake enter from the drain, knowing he had little time left to live but hoping he would somehow break free.

The young python backed out of the side tunnel into the drain and proceeded in the direction that he had been going before he slipped in the tunnel after the young rat. He had satisfied one of his requirements with the killing and eating of the rat which, fortunately, hadn't put up too much of a fight to bother him. One butt of his hard head had crushed the young rats head and allowed him to unhinge his jaws and swallow it whole. The rat lay slightly heavier than he would have wanted at this time, as it would take a whole week for him to consume it, but he had needed the strength which it would give him while he slept. All he needed now was some warmth and sunshine after his soaking. Already he was getting warmed up from the trickle of sun-heated water that was flowing through the drain. Onward he went, looking for the tell-tale spot of light that would tell him that he was coming to the end of the underground portion of the drain, eventually allowing him to get into the sunshine.

CHAPTER 5

Monna had lain contentedly all day, dozing and occasionally cleaning her new born kittens by licking them clean with her tongue, after they had suckled. The rough-cleaning tongue of their mother also helped the blind, helpless little bodies to digest the milk that they had managed to extract from her and it also served to comfort them by letting them know where their mother was and where to find the warm body that they could snuggle into.

It was early evening and Monna needed to go outside again to see if she could catch, or find, some food to eat. She also needed a drink as she hadn't moved all day away from her kittens. They had just had a meal not long ago and had been thoroughly cleaned. They were now pressed close to her tummy, one sprawled across the other's body. Monna rose quietly, stopping to see if her new-born moved after her body heat had moved away from them, but not one twitch did she observe. So off she went into the cooling evening. With no further rain that day the early evening was alive with activity. Moths danced around the porch light that Margot had switched on for Tony to see to park the car. Chit chats scampered after insects that alighted on walls and roofs. The wooded areas around the house hummed with the noise from beating insect wings and cricket songs. Only when danger was thought to be near was this night song ever silenced, then immediately picked up again when everything was found to be alright.

Monna had a look at Smudge's plate but he had left nothing that night, having been so hungry, after losing so much of his morning meal that he had even licked the plate clean. Monna had heard him as he licked his plate. He had licked so hard that the plate had been moving and rattling around on the porch. She moved out from the house towards the road that ran through Goodwood Hill, where workmen had been repairing its surface and found the remains of one of the men's dinners which was wrapped in heavy greaseproof paper. After having unravelled the twisted paper to get to the meal she found it had mainly consisted of fried rice with prawns, squid and vegetables. Smudge would not have eaten this, being a domesticated home cat used to humans supplying him with cat food, but to Monna it was a special delight as she was used to having less than this and sometimes only what she could pick out of garbage bags. Monna tucked into the remains of the road repairman's leftover meal and almost had to force herself to eat the last mouthful. Having eaten till she was almost bursting, Monna decided to explore her new home area as she wandered down towards her drinking place at the bottom garden drain. She skirted the house, watching Smudge through the open French doors as she passed. Smudge was running from one to the other begging for some of Tony and Margot's evening meal as they sat at the dining table. The soft murmur of their conversation drifted out to her alert ears, as Tony commented on Smudge appearing to be quite hungry and suggesting that maybe Margot should increase the amount of his cat food. Margot agreed as she was finding him to be a bit of a nuisance at the table and it was quite unlike him. Their conversation drifted away in the evening air as Monna continued her inspection, always heading towards the drain at the bottom of the garden where she knew there would be the cooling drink of cold water she now wanted.

Eventually she reached her drinking place as she made her way down into the drain where the water was murmuring into the little pool, protected from the sunshine by the overhanging bushes and grasses, just before it flowed into the dark underground drain on its way to the sea. As she lapped she watched the dark maw of the drain warily but, not a thing was there, nor any scent to bother her. There had been a rat family in there but the scent was old so she knew they no longer lived in the underground position of the drain. Having finished her drink, she clambered out of her drinking place and strolled up the garden towards the tree that lead to her home and kittens. She had almost reached the tree when she saw Smudge streaking towards her from the house. Swiftly, she dived for the bole of the tree in an effort to reach the roof where she could protect her young ones from this strange cat. She reached the tree second before Smudge did. Smudge saw the female cat reach the tree but he couldn't stop. He saw the glint of light on her paws as she unsheathed her claws and swiped swiftly at his head. He managed to get his head out of the road but her paw caught him on the leg that was outstretched to take his weight on his next stride. His leg crumpled beneath him and he went flat on his nose into the root of the tree. Eyes watering with pain, he jumped up to his feet to be confronted by a furious arched back female cat perched on the bole of the sloping tree. A hiss of fury came from Monna. No male tom cat was going to get near her kittens!

13

Smudge was very surprised at the furious she-cat who stood defensively before him with her fur sticking out and back arched. This was his home. She was the intruder, she should have been running away. That's what all the other cats had done who had ventured into his domain, but there she stood all ready to give battle. Smudge took a step forward toward her and another hiss of warning and fury resounded in his ears. Impasse was struck. He couldn't walk away and ignore her, neither could he move forward into the path of the lethal looking claws so he just stood there looking to her. As time passed she knew he was not going to attack so she allowed the arch in her back and upright fur to return to their normal position. Slowly she backed further up the tree slope away from him until the tree bole started to straighten out and she could back up no further. Inching her body round, but still keeping her eyes facing him, she eventually manoeuvred her position on the tree bole till she was facing up the tree with her head still facing toward the tom cat. He hadn't moved one inch while she completed her manoeuvres as it was one thing to fight a strange cat in his domain but an entirely different thing to face and fight a furious female cat protecting her young. Smudge was really quite pleased to have got off so lightly and would be glad when she released him from those angry eyes. Monna quickly turned her head and sprang up the tree to stop on the branch leading to the roof and her home. She eyed Smudge again from this vantage point but he still hadn't made a move. She stood there watching him closely for a while until he slowly moved forward to the tree, sniffed at the place she had been standing, then turned and walked away. Not once had he allowed their eyes to meet as he had looked in her general direction. He had just stood very still waiting for her to go up the tree before he had sniffed at the tree bole.

Monna watched him go back into the house before making her way to the kittens she had been prepared to protect with her life, and settled down for another night.

CHAPTER 6

The days went past, with the occasional confrontation between Monna and Smudge which Monna usually won with her spitting fury. Gradually both adult cats became used to each other and tried to avoid meeting. Smudge, with Margo's extra food, would leave enough for Monna and make sure he was nowhere around when she climbed down from the roof of the house. Monna was now eating twice a day the cat food that normal domestic cats received from their owners so she was beginning to put on some weight. This would all have been fine if it wasn't for the fact that her nose began to run and her head ached. She wasn't aware of it but she had caught the 'flu with her two day journey to find a home.

The two kittens grew bigger and bigger on the rich milk from their mother, who no longer had to scrounge for food. First their eyes opened a few days after their birth, then they started to grow fur around their tubby little bodies. The male, Shu, was orange in colour, like the father he would never know. The female, Pen, was the same dark colour of her mother, without the white patch above her right eye. Shu was adventurous, always making for the entrance to the home, to get out into the bright light that he could see beyond. Monna had to keep a watchful eye on him and drag him back whenever she caught him heading for the sunshine and the roof. Pen was the opposite, she was content to stay as far away from the entrance as possible and was far from happy when her mother had to go out and leave them alone. When this happened she tended to back into the furthest place away from the entrance that she could get. By the time Monna had decided to bring the first gecko to allow her kittens to see solid food, Shu was the dominant one of the two. Monna entered with the lizard hanging from her mouth and Shu immediately ran forward to take it from her. She wouldn't let him and took it toward Pen but she backed away from her mother wondering what was hanging from her mouth. Monna placed it in front of

Pen but she would have nothing to do with it. Shu however walked right up to it and sniffed at the body of the gecko, his natural instincts took over and he grabbed it in his teeth, pulling it after him, growling under his breath. Monna stepped forward and placed her paw on the body of the gecko. This only made Shu sink his teeth into the body and try all the harder to pull the gecko away from under his mother's paw. He was very surprised when the part of the body that he had in his teeth came away and he was left with it in his mouth. He liked the taste of the flesh and juices he found in his mouth and swallowed. His mother had by now removed her paw from the body and he went back to try and get another part to swallow. Pen watched him closely and went toward him to see what he was doing but Shu warned her not to approach with a long low growl. Pen stood where she was and watched him until he had had enough of worrying what remained of the gecko. When he left she then went over and closed her mouth on the body as she had seen do and was pleasantly surprised at the taste in her mouth. She timidly tore off a piece, just like Shu, and swallowed. It was nice so she consumed what was left of the gecko body. Over the next day or two the pattern remained the same, Shu ate most of the catch that his mother brought in and if there was anything left when he was finished then Pen was allowed to eat. If Shu ate the whole catch then Pen went hungry and only got the milk from her mother. With the meat going into his body Shu got bigger and bigger but Pen remained much smaller as she was mainly only getting milk from her mum.

The bigger Shu got the more he pushed Pen around till she spent most of her time as far away from him as possible in the back of the home, never venturing toward the front of the entrance.

CHAPTER 7

Monna's 'flu was getting worse. She was forever going down to the drinking spot at the drain to swallow some cool liquid down her fiery throat. She was getting around now quite freely as she and Smudge tended to ignore each other. Smudge occasionally chased her when he had had a bad day but all in all they lived a quiet co-existence. The kittens were getting bigger and Shu would poke his head out from under the eaves of the roof to see what was going on but Pen would only have a look outside during the evening light as she didn't like to look in the bright sunlight.

Monna was down at the drinking place lapping at the cool, cool water to ease the fire that burned in her throat. She was watching the dark hole of the drain where it vanished into the ground, as usual, watching for any movement within. She knew this was the only dangerous spot in the garden as she had searched diligently around the house and its building and found nothing. As she drank her fill she watched the entrance closely. Her ears pricked up. She could hear a strange rushing sound getting louder and louder. The sound didn't come from ahead of her but from above. She jumped to the side, scrambling, for a grip on the surface of the drain as her head snapped towards the sky. What she saw made her all the more frantic in her movements until she lost her footing and plunged into the pool of drinking water at the bottom of the drain. The hawk was using his wings to break his plunge toward the cat that had suddenly ended up in the water. There was no quick catch for him today. Wings beating frantically he was managing to get some distance from the ground as he moved swiftly above the spot that Monna has been a minute ago. With a steadier beat of his wings he was starting to rise away from the ground and the garden, higher and higher, till he was above the trees again. The sun caught him in its grasp showing his fine plumage of light brown body, with black flight feathers and proud head with full white throat. Up and up he went watching for another prey that might not get away. He was quite young and inexperienced so there was no disgrace in not catching the cat. Monna meantime was out of the water and dashing for the safety of the roof home where her kittens were. Smudge looked on, amazed at her speed when there was no one chasing her. Why should she run so fast away from nothing? Smudge, of course, hadn't seen the hawk attack and was mystified at Monna's flight.

The hawk, meanwhile, was slowly soaring round and round effortlessly, above the clearing that held the next house down the road. His sharp eyes were glued to the ground and surrounding area above this patch in the woods. He was just in the point of swinging over toward the next clearing when he saw a movement in the sunshine. Close inspection showed him a python curled up and basking in the sun at the edge of a drain.

The young hawk hovered, wings flaying into the air to stop all forward movement as he took in the scene that his eyes told him was an easy catch. No other danger was there, so he closed his wings half into his body and dived toward the python. The python's senses told him there was something fast coming in his direction even before the little holes in the side of his head, which were his ears, told him. His head shot from the coiled position it had been on his body toward the sky, striking the body of the young hawk even as he had just brought his feet forward with claws ready to clutch the python.

Knocked off balance with the blow to his side he plunged in a tangle of feathers, wings, feet and body onto the ground, struggling to get to his feet. The python took in this entire scene and decided that this foe was too big for him to tackle as it looked to be the size of a full grown chicken with very sharp claws, so he took off heading for the security of the drain and the dark out of the sunlight. The young hawk meanwhile had got to his feet, none the worse for his contact with the ground, and watched his meal crawl into the dark opening in the drain. He ruffled his feathers into place and launched himself once more into the sky with eyes blazing at having missed another meal. Two in one day would not do and he resolved to do better next time. Monna and Shu had watched the hawk plunge to the ground from the safety of their home under the roof of Tony and Margot's house. As they watched he rose back into the sky with no catch and slowly swung away from their home to search further down the road. Monna ushered Shu back inside and decided that she would not go out again today. She was soaking wet after her unexpected bath in the drinking pool and started to lick herself dry, with a little help from her two kittens.

The python meanwhile was moving up through the drain looking for any sign of another rat which he could eat as he was beginning to find that he was feeling quite hungry now, having had nothing to eat in a fortnight since he last managed to catch a meal.

CHAPTER 8

Monna was getting worse, her nose was running constantly, her eyes itched and watered and her head was aching continuously. She was forever running to the drinking hole to ease the fire in her throat. She decided it was time to take her family away from the home in the roof – it was getting too small anyway since her family was getting bigger in size – and take them to the jungle area at the drain where they would get more chance at catching insects and she would be nearer the drain so she could get a drink quicker. Monna moved out of the den in the roof "meowing" encouragement to her kittens to come after her. Shu didn't hesitate and scampered after her but Pen remained at the back of the den waiting for her mother to come back, she had no intention of leaving this warm dark hole that had been her home all her little life. Monna tried all she knew to get Pen out of the den but to no avail. She decided to bring Shu down the tree to the ground and proceeded to catch him in her teeth by the scruff of loose skin and fur on his neck. She could hardly breath with his fur in her nose and mouth but she picked him up and jumped onto the branch, making her way along and down onto the ground. As she put him down on the grass at the bottom of the tree she had to sneeze to clear her nose so she could breathe easier. Her head ached, her neck muscles ached and her throat was on fire again. Normally she would have gone straight back up to their home under the roof and dragged Pen out by the scruff of her neck to get her down to the ground along with her brother but she was so sore and thirsty that she decided to go for a drink first before she tackled this job. Signalling Shu to stay where he was she scampered off down the garden, down into the drinking hole. The run had made her head even worse and she sneezed again before she put her head down to get her much needed drink.

The python heard the sneeze and knew that his next meal was in front of him. He eased his way forward to the front of the drain hole and saw the cat lapping greedily at the water. Monna would normally have spied the movement in the dark maw of the drain but her 'flu made her ache so much that her suspicious watchfulness was abandoned. She never knew what happened as the python's hard mouth hit her in the head and crushed her skull. She died with the thought of how wonderful the water was and how cooling to her throat.

CHAPTER 9

Shu was having a great time scampering about the bole of the tree. First he would dive at a blade of grass that moved in the wind then he would show fear and scamper halfway back up the tree bole. When curiosity got the better of him again he would plunge back to the ground and attack another blade of moving grass.

Smudge sauntered round the corner of the house and stopped short when he saw Shu playing at the base of the she-cat's tree. "Oh no", he thought "not another one", but it dawned on him quite quickly that this must be one of the she-cat's kittens. This was the first he had seen of them and he wondered how many there were. He looked around searching to see if he could spy Monna anywhere close. He knew that if she found him near her kittens that she would see him off with her sharp claws and furious spitting. Nowhere could he see the mother of this kitten so he eased himself forward toward Shu. The little kitten got the fright of his life when he eventually noticed Smudge coming toward him and shot as far up the tree bole as his little legs would get him. This strange car was big! Much bigger than his mother and his colours of mainly white with black patches seemed to make him appear bigger the nearer he got to the tree. Shu "meowed" plaintively, but quietly, calling for his mother. Smudge stopped, alert for the familiar rush of female cat, dashing to rescue her kitten. Time passed and the mother cat didn't appear. Shu continued to "meow" quietly while searching for sight of his mum. Where could she be? She always came running when he called but Monna would never again answer the call of her frightened son. After some time had passed Smudge continued toward the tree where the little kitten was. He quite liked what he saw of this strange little fellow and had no intention of hurting him. He just wanted a closer look at this orange coloured little visitor. "Meow" he said as a greeting and Shu scrabbled all the more on the tree bole, trying to get higher. "Meow" said Smudge and caused more scrabbling on the tree bole. Shu was trying so hard to get up the tree backwards and away from this big cat that his little claws missed their mark and down he tumbled, landing at Smudge's feet. He lay dazedly in a ball and for a minute didn't know what had happened. By the time he could react Smudge had leaned down and was sniffing him all over. Shu lay very still as he didn't know what to make of this big almost white monster standing over him sniffing.

Smudge could smell the mother cat, Shu himself and one other female cat so he knew that the she-cat had two kittens. He looked around again for the mother but still she was nowhere in sight. He looked about for the other kitten but couldn't see her either. By this time Shu had begun to get his courage back and hissed at the big cat from his position on the ground. Smudge just ignored him and continued to look around for the others. Shu scrambled to his feet and sniffed the big cat the same way he had been sniffed. He obviously wasn't familiar but the scent wasn't unpleasant either. Shu began to gain more and more confidence. He jumped away playfully then bounced back to pounce on Smudge's tail, which was lying on the ground. Smudge twitched his tail out of the way and Shu bolted for the tree again only to bound back to catch the tail.

The kitten continued to run to Smudge's tail, bite it then dive away up the tree. Smudge was beginning to get more and more annoyed at the kitten's games and his tail twitched furiously, trying to show that he didn't like it being bitten. But Shu didn't understand and as the tail twitching increased, he chased it all the more. Finally, Smudge could stand it no more and swiped the kitten with his sheathed paw knocking him head over tail into the tree. Shu sat dumbfounded at this attack while Smudge walked away back toward the house with his tail still twitching vigorously. Shu gained his feet again and looked around to see if this mother had come back but she was nowhere in sight.

Night time came and still no mother. Shu by this time was getting a bit afraid and hungry. Where could she be? He decided he should go back the den in the roof where his sister still was but found he couldn't climb the tree. He sat miserably on the bole of the tree every now and then giving a plaintive call for his mother came back but he knew there would be no food without her. The lightning flashed across the sky causing Shu to jump with alarm. The flash had all the promise of a large downpour of rain for that evening and the resulting crash of thunder brought Margot's attention to the impending storm so that instead of putting Smudge's evening meal outside she decided to feed him in the kitchen that night. This was unlucky for Shu as he might have found what was left of Smudge's dinner, just like his mum, but since Smudge was fed inside that night neither he, nor Pen, had anything to eat.

CHAPTER 10

The torrential rain lasted half the night. Shu tried but could not find anywhere dry to hide near the tree bole. He hadn't wanted to leave the area where his mother had left him before she went away. She hadn't returned but he reasoned he should just stay where he was as this would be the place that his mother would look for him. As the moon finally managed to break through the rain soaked clouds that were passing overhead they shone on a saturated kitten crouched in the grass at the foot of the tree. His ginger fur was dark and lank with the soaking it had had and a more miserable little kitten had never before been seen in moonlight.

Pen meanwhile had been hiding in their home while the lightning had flashed and the thunder rolled across the night sky. Now that the rain had stopped and her fear had gone she could feel her hunger rising again. She cautiously moved to the entrance and peaked out. She could see the moonlight playing on the trees and roof of the house but nowhere could she see her mother or brother. She gave a plaintive "meow" and heard the answering call from her brother. She meowed again and heard the rapid scrape of small claws on the tree bole as Shu tried to rush up toward her. Shu never made it as he only got half way when the strength of his legs and the precarious position he was in let him down so that he had to jump to the ground before he fell. Shu called to Pen to come down to him. He tried to climb again but had to jump to the ground once more as his little claws lost purchase on the tree bole. Both kittens were hungry and lonely being apart and called to each other and for their mum who wouldn't come.

CHAPTER 11

Tony was telling Margot about the terrible storm and how he had thought he had heard cats meowing during the night outside in the yard. Margot hadn't heard a thing during her night as she had lain contentedly sleeping. Smudge knew the mother cat had brought one of her little ones down to the ground and he suspected that she had brought the other one down too. Tony made up Smudge's meal as Margot made his breakfast before they both headed off to do whatever it was they were doing that day.

Tony placed Smudge's meal outside on the porch as he always did and had a look around to see if he could spy any strange cats around. He didn't notice the still damp kitten with the rain darkened ginger fur as it hid on the side of the tree furthest away from him. Smudge was placed outside on the porch after having made a nuisance of himself at the breakfast table begging for some of Tony's meal. Smudge went to his own plate and consumed what he wanted of his meal before proceeding on his wandering for that day.

Shu watched him go from his hiding spot and when he was out of sight he edged round the tree bole and followed his nose toward the smell of food that had been drifting toward him on the slowly heating air as the sun got higher and higher. Pen could smell the food also and eased her head out of the den in the roof to see if it was anywhere near her. This was the first day she had ventured outside but hunger had overcome her fear.

Shu reached Smudge's plate and proceeded to eat his fill. Pen could only stand on the roof and meow miserably. When Shu was finished he wandered out into the garden to play without a thought for his sister who kept calling for their mother or him. Occasionally he would call for his mother but for the most part he played quite happily. When he did spy Smudge during the day he ran away and hid as he remembered the striking paw which knocked him into the ground and he didn't want a repeat of the blow.

Smudge ignored both Shu and Pen up on the roof but he was fully aware that he had not seen hide nor hair of the mother cat since yesterday. Shu had found a nice place under the annex building where he could hide when he saw Smudge around so he stayed quite close to the tree, the main house and the annex buildings. Pen could see her brother sometimes as he played around the house but there was no way she could get down to him and he didn't seem to take much notice of her anyway. When she saw the big white cat with the dark smudges she ran back into the den and hid for a little while before venturing back out. She had tried to catch the fast moving geckos but they had been too quick for her so she was still very, very hungry.

When Margot drove into the yard from the road she spied the little dark kitten diving into a place on the roof. When Margot had finished getting her messages away she went outside and tried to see where the kitten had vanished and could just see the little head poke out from the roof occasionally.

When Tony came in that night she told him of what she had seen. "There" he said, "I told you I had heard cats last night during the storm". Margot kept pestering him to do something about it so of he went to fetch his ladders. As he made his way back he spied a flash of orange streaking through a hole in the boarding of the annex building. "Margot", he shouted, "was it an orange kitten you saw today?" Margot came to the door of the kitchen and told him it had been a dark kitten she had seen and not an orange one. "Well, I've just seen an orange one heading under the building down there", he said pointing towards the annex building where Shu had vanished when he saw the big tall thing that walked on two legs instead of four. "Then there must be two of them", was Margot's observation. "Or maybe more than two", said Tony under his breath so that Margot couldn't hear him.

Tony placed his ladder against the porch roof and climbed up to see if he could see the dark kitten that was supposed to be under the eaves of the roof. His hand wouldn't reach into the space between the house roof and the porch roof so he clambered back down to fetch a torch to see if he could see anything.

When he returned he could see the hole that had made a home for the mother cat and her kittens but it was so deep and so far in that he couldn't see if the kittens were there at all. Pen was as far back as she could go and watched fearfully as the bright beam of light from the torch swept the entrance to the den. Tony went back down the ladders and made up a small dish of cat food, telling Margot that maybe the smell of the food would bring out any little kittens that were up on the roof hiding so that he could catch them.

He placed the dish of food down on the porch roof and made soothing sounds to allay the kitten's fears. After waiting half an hour, with no sign of any kittens coming into the open for the food on the roof, Tony went back down the ladder leaving the plate, with the rich smell, where he had placed it. Tony told Margot he would check the plate after he had had dinner to see if any had been taken.

When Pen sensed that the man-thing had left and gone inside the house she sneaked cautiously out of the den into the warm evening. Her mouth was watering as she smelled the cat meat that Tony had placed on a plate. This was the smell that had taunted her yesterday when she was hungry and couldn't get down to where Shu was having something to eat. Pen gobbled down the contents of the plate into her hollow tummy. This food was good and she didn't even have to fight Shu for a share of it. When she had finished she walked quietly over to the small pool of water that still had not evaporated from the house roans after the previous evening's rainfall and drank her fill. Having satisfied her thirst Pen crept into the den and placed herself as far back from the entrance as possible before curling herself into a ball prepared for a night sleep.

Tony found an empty plate when he climbed the ladder after having his evening meal. Again he switched on the powerful beam of his torch into the space beneath the roof and this time was rewarded with a frightened "Meow" and hissing. Pen had been rudely awakened by the bright light shining into the den and had got such a fright that she had let out a frantic call before arching her back and hissing at this bright intruder.

Tony tried coaxing the kitten out of the hole so he could catch it but eventually he knew that he could stand there all night and he would have no success. Tony put away the ladders and placed a broad board against the roof to give the little kitten an easy passage down to the ground. He then went in the house to tell Margot what he had heard and done. Later on Margot made up another dish of cat food and asked Tony to go and place it where he thought the other kitten would be able to get it. Tony decided to place it on the porch where they normally placed Smudge's dish as he wanted to bring the little orange kitten out from his hiding place under the annex building.

Sure enough, when Tony and Margot were asleep that night Shu came out from his hiding place and had a lovely meal on his very own dish.

Days went passed and Tony and Margot continued to lay out food for the two kittens. Tony always spent some time trying to get Pen to come out of her hiding place but she would never venture forth. Shu on the other hand had started to go to the back door of the porch when he was hungry and meow for food. When he heard anyone moving behind the door he would always run to the tree bole and watch from there as Tony or Margot placed down the dish with his food in it.

CHAPTER 12

Pen was getting used to having her meals placed outside the entrance of what she now considered to be her home and by extension was beginning to trust Tony who supplied her food. In truth she looked forward to him coming at meal times. He was the only company she had each day and he spent his time, while she ate, talking to her and making funny noises which she did not understand. She only knew he was nice and as days passed she trusted him more and more.

The only problem, which had not been an issue before was water. Tony always supplied food but never thought of water. The food he supplied was cat food and it was moist so he never thought about water.

He had never seen Smudge drinking water so in his mind the cat food provided all that was required. He did not know that Smudge used the same drinking place at the bottom of the garden that Pen's mother had used.

When her mum had been around her mother's milk had quenched her thirst but her mother no longer came when she called and had not been anywhere close since the last time she had seen her at least three days ago.

Now she had to find puddles of rain water which were few and far between even though it was Singapore's rainy season. There was liquid in the meals that Tony left but she still found she was thirsty during the day or night and would have to search for water on the roof.

Shu however was getting on with Smudge and growing quite healthy like a normal domestic kitten. He was also interacting with Smudge more and more -jumping out of hiding places as Smudge sauntered by and jumping on his back or trying to grab the swishing tail as Smudge passed .

One night Tony came home and announced to Margot that he had been picked to play for the home team at the Cricket Club next Saturday morning and that she should get her glad rags on as they would be having there evening meal at the club. This was exciting news as it was not often that Tony had time off for playing. So come the Saturday Tony went off to play cricket and Margot tidied up after lunch and prepared for the evening at the Cricket Club. Halfway through the afternoon the telephone rang and it was the Club Captain to tell Margot that there had been an accident and the Tony had broken a bone in his leg and was in hospital. Margot dropped everything and headed off to see Tony in hospital. It turned out the break was not too bad but it meant that Tony would have to be very careful on what he was doing and of course would need to have a set of crutches to get around.

Pen did not find a meal outside her home that night nor for many nights to come because Tony couldn't climb the ladder onto the roof. With no food and little water Pen was in a desperate position. She could hear Shu getting his meals from Margot but of course Margot could not carry or climb the ladder to give a much required bowl of food to Pen.

Chasing after geckos was hard work and she had not had to do it up till now as her mum had provided before her disappearance and Tony had provided after that.

So after a couple of days Pen was very, very hungry and thirsty. She could hear Shu down at the bole of the tree very closeby. She had missed his company since her mum had left and listening to him now jumping around she felt lonely, depressed, hungry and very thirsty. So she decided to leave her home in the roof and see if she could join Shu at the bottom of the great tree.

Tentatively she crawled across the roof toward the great tree branch she had watched her mother use to get to the bottom of the tree and which her brother had failed to climb. As she got to the position below the branch she almost gave up and wanted to return to her home under the roof but taking courage in her small body she leapt upward and found herself clawing up onto the branch. Once secure it was an easy walk to the bole of the great tree and, with Shu now watching his sister, she easily scrambled down the tree to be met by her brother in a rush of playful joy.

Pen could smell the food on the porch at the back door where Margot had placed Shu and Smudge's food bowls. Both had left food in each bowl that they had not wanted. Pen was so hungry that she ignored her brother's attempts to play-hug and went to the bowls of food and scoffed the lot. That night Margot saw the empty bowls and suspected that there had been more than Smudge and Shu at feeding there. So she put out a third bowl of food the next night and watched from behind the kitchen door. Soon she saw a third kitten join her orange brother at the bowl of cat food which she could tell was the one that Tony always placed outside her home under the roof of the house.

Margot knew it was Pen who had joined the group as her fur colouring was the same as Tony had described when he had first ventured onto the roof where Monna had found refuge from the storm. So from that night on a third bowl was placed along with the others and Smudge, Shu and Pen ate their meals together.

When Tony got back from the hospital he was quite worried about Pen as he knew he would not be able to climb the ladder to give her some food and he was very glad after he heard Margot's tale of the third cat at the porch feeding area where three bowls were laid out daily.

Over the coming days Pen got used to both her human friends who fed her and her brother. Both kittens now pursued Smudge as a target for their ambushes and tail attacks. Tony and Margot had many laughs and chuckles at both their antics.

CHAPTER 13

Meanwhile Boh the hawk had become much more active and successful in his hunting prowess, and was regularly seen wheeling about the tall buildings before stooping for a kill. He did not miss the flash of ginger fur as Shu ran into the bushes and jungle-like undergrowth but he knew that to close his wings and chase after the ginger cat would place him in danger so near to the house, so he continued to circle around his area and kept his eyes open for an easier and safer target like a pigeon or some other bird taking flight from the buildings or trees in his patch of Singapore.

Boh was unaware that the reason he had observed the ginger flash of colour was that Shu was on his way to the bottom of the garden to get a sip of water at the open water area, just as it disappeared back underground and where his mother had vanished the night she went for a drink and left him at the bole of the great tree.

It was Smudge who had shown him the place to get a drink of water whenever he felt thirsty but Smudge was not thirsty that day so Shu had gone on his own. He had seen the dark hole where the water had gone underground and even though he knew nothing of the snake that had killed his mother he was still quite fearful of that dark hole that seemed to swallow the water as it left the sunlight.

After his drink Shu returned to the house area to play with Pen and Smudge but just as he got there Tony drove into the front yard, circled the great tree and parked his car as usual. Shu was very fearful of the car and the noise that it made and his reaction was to run away and hide. Pen and Smudge on the other hand were quite glad to hear the sound of the engine as they knew that this would lead to them getting their daily bowl of food at the back door leading to the kitchen. Sometime later Shu would appear at his own bowl and consume what he wished of the contents, which was getting less and less, as he was now hunting in the undergrowth for anything that he decided was good to eat.

CHAPTER 14

One day Tony arrived home and informed Margot that he was being posted to Kuala Lumpur in Malaysia.

They had only a couple of days for Tony to head there and Margot would follow on as quickly as she could. This meant that they had to inform the leasing agent, get the furniture packed and ready to head up to Kuala Lumpur, carry out the inventory of the house and Tony had to find himself an agent in Malaysia who could meet with Margot when she arrived city and show her houses or apartments to rent.

It was no wonder that with all the rushing around Margot forgot about the cats and it was not till a day or two before they left with the furniture that Margot thought about what would happen to Smudge, Shu and Pen.

She called her neighbours on both sides of the area to see if they wanted two young cats. Since Smudge was their cat he would go with them but Shu and Pen were a different matter. However, nobody wanted the two little ones.

Margot spoke to Tony on the phone and they decided that they would have to take Shu and Pen with them as well as Smudge.

So on the morning that Margot had to hand in the keys to the house she went out and picked up Smudge then Pen and placed them in travel boxes. However Shu was nowhere to be found. She searched and searched but could not find him and the time eventually ran out with the furniture truck already on its journey to Malaysia.

Margot had to get the keys to the leasing agent firm before she caught her flight to Kuala Lumpur to meet up with Tony.

She was very sad at having to leave without Shu but she really had no option. None of the neighbours had wanted any of her cats and she had no idea where Shu was. She told the agent about it when she handed in the keys and asked them to ask the new tenants to look out for Shu and to make sure he was fed.

CHAPTER 15

Shu had gone hunting in the wooded area of Goodwood Hill Road that day and having caught and consumed his morning meal had found a quiet sunny spot in the undergrowth and had fallen fast asleep.

As it was getting dark he woke up and decided he would go back to the house and have the meal that either Tony or Margot had lain out for him as they did every day for himself, Pen and Smudge.

He approached the house quite happily and was looking forward to seeing his sister but as he got closer he realised it was in darkness and there was no sign of the other cats. Jumping up on the porch he approached the back door area where the bowls of food were always left - but again he was disappointed as no bowls were visible.

He just did not understand what was happening. There was always at least one bowl left out at the feeding place but tonight there was none. And where were Smudge and Pen? There should at least be one of them hanging around the house.

As time went on he became more concerned about the absence of the other cats than he was about the lack of food. Where could Smudge and Pen have gone and why were there no bowls left out on the porch?

Night turned into day then night again and there was still no sign of Smudge or Pen. By now Shu was very worried. There had also been no lights or movement in the house and no cars coming into the garden.

New people arrived with a flurry of activity and when Shu approached they shouted at him and threw stones in an attempt to chase him away. So Shu retreated to the undergrowth at the side of the drive into the house to ponder what he should do next.

As he sat there he heard the barking of a dog and out of the front door of the house shot a medium size dog with brown and white fur, teeth showing and barking furiously as it rushed toward the place where Shu was sitting. Shu did not hesitate and scrambled across the drive to the bole of the great tree. Claws gripped the bark and Shu was clawing his way up the tree bole and out over the house drive on the branch that led to the porch roof. Meanwhile the brown and white dog , unable to climb the tree, was left barking with his front paws on the trunk of the tree and his back feet on the house driveway, eyes searching for the cat he had smelled and saw in his new abode.

Later that night Shu tried to go to the back door of the house where he would normally find the bowl of food left out for him and the others, but the dog went into a frenzy in the house barking and growling and claws scratching at the back door. So Shu ran and hid in the undergrowth.

Next day Shu spent the day hunting and sleeping in the sunshine but when he returned to the house the dog got angry again and made a horrible noise with all the barking and scratching at the door so much so that Shu left and went in to the undergrowth for the night.

This went on for a week till Shu stopped going near the house and just stayed in the bottom half of the garden. He could look after himself. He considered this to be his home and he knew the place very well. He knew where he would be able to catch his food and also the place where he could get a drink at the bottom of the garden where his Mum, Pen, Smudge and himself used as it was the only place in the area that the water surfaced for a short distance before going back underground.

CHAPTER 16

Boh had seen Shu a number of times but had not attempted to catch him as he hadn't been hungry then. But Boh had made note of the fact that Shu went to the bottom of the garden to get a drink and some day he would be hungry enough to attack the ginger coloured cat.

On the particular day the young python was very, very hungry as he had not had a meal in weeks, not since the fatal day he had caught Monna. So from his safe place in the drain he had edged back to the opening in the hope of catching a bird having a drink. As he lay there, just inside the drain opening, he spied Shu coming down to the place where he always stood for a drink.

The python drew himself together in readiness for a strike at the ginger cat who he hoped would be his meal for today.

Boh was also hungry and had spied the ginger cat on his way down to the opening in the drain where Boh had seem him many a time having a drink of water. He waited till Shu had crouched down at the water's edge with his head down as he drank, then he swooped with his legs in front and claws extended.

Shu heard the noise of the wind rushing through the Boh's feathers and jumped to the side just as the python's head and half his body shot from the dark edge of the drain to the place where he had been drinking.

As the python was at the full stretch of his lunge, Boh had his legs way out in front of his body and was fully committed to grab the ginger cat. But the cat was no longer in its place and his claws reacted and closed fully into the body of the python - who was somehow in the same place the cat had been.

The python reacted with a full hiss of rage and pain and the rest of his body emerged and wrapped itself around the struggling bird. Boh's claws went fully into the flesh of the python and his beak struck again and again at the python's head.

The python was using the muscles of his young body to try and crush the hawk to death but the blows to his head were interfering with the messages from his head to his body. He was getting weaker and weaker and Boh's strikes where getting stronger and stronger

Boh tried and managed to extract his wings from the coils of the young python and with great beats of his wings took to the air with the python still clutched in his talons. The young python still kept striking at the hawks head and eventually Boh had to retract his claws from the flesh of the snake. On releasing the python he surged up into the sky and the python plunged to the ground and bounced twice before coming to a rest in the grass. In just a few seconds he had slithered into the undergrowth.

Shu, who had watched all this from the undergrowth where he had hidden, crawled back out into the garden. He looked up at Boh, who was flying higher and higher, then he turned and looked at the place where the python had escaped into and watched the tail of the python disappear.

Shu shook himself and decided that enough was enough. He would leave this garden that he had known as his home and go out into the wide world. So, with a quick look skyward to see the disappearing bird and a further look at the place where the tail had disappeared, Shu shook himself and sauntered off into the undergrowth looking for a new place to live and possibly, if he was lucky, some new friends.

THE END

ABOUT THE AUTHOR

George Spence has always had a love of animals and has told animal tales since ever he can remember. He has been known for rescuing ill creatures, most famously injured pigeons that he nursed back to health – many birds have him to thank for his care including Misty, Lucky and the rather unfortunate Not-So-Lucky for whom he once stopped a double decker bus. He enjoyed a wonderful career rising through the ranks of aircraft engineer to become Maintenance Manager for Air Canada – a job that took him around the world along the way. In the 1980s he was stationed in Singapore and this is where the story of Monna, Shu, Pen and Smudge was born – at the home of real friends Margot and Tony. George is husband to Sheena, father to Pamela and Papa to Ruben and lives in the beautiful West Coast of Scotland.

Printed in Great Britain
by Amazon

71899470R00026